VALENTINES FOR EVERYONE

Written by Cecilia Minden and Joanne Meier • Illustrated by Bob Ostrom
Created by Herbie J. Thorpe

ABOUT THE AUTHORS

Cecilia Minden, PhD, is the former director of the Language and Literacy Program at the Harvard Graduate School of Education. She is now a reading consultant for school and library publications. She earned her PhD in reading education from the University of Virginia. Cecilia and her husband, Dave Cupp, live outside Chapel Hill, North Carolina. They enjoy sharing their love of reading with their grandchildren, Chelsea and Qadir.

Joanne Meier, PhD, has worked as an elementary school teacher, university professor, and researcher. She earned her BA in early childhood education from the University of South Carolina, and her MEd and PhD in education from the University of Virginia. She currently works as a literacy consultant for schools and private organizations. Joanne lives in Virginia with her husband Eric, daughters Kella and Erin, two cats, and a gerbil.

ABOUT THE ILLUSTRATOR

Bob Ostrom has been illustrating children's books for nearly twenty years. A graduate of the New England School of Art & Design at Suffolk University, Bob has worked for such companies as Disney, Nickelodeon, and Cartoon Network. He lives in North Carolina with his wife Melissa and three children, Will, Charlie, and Mae.

ABOUT THE SERIES CREATOR

Herbie J. Thorpe had long envisioned a beginning-readers' series about a fun, energetic bear with a big imagination. Herbie is a book lover and an avid supporter of libraries and the role they play in fostering the love of reading. He consults with librarians and matches them with the perfect books for their students and patrons. He lives in Louisiana with his wife Misty and their daughter Carson.

The Child's World®

Published in the United States of America by The Child's World®
1980 Lookout Drive • Mankato, MN 56003-1705
800-599-READ • www.childsworld.com

Acknowledgments
The Child's World®: Mary Berendes, Publishing Director
The Design Lab: Kathleen Petelinsek, Design;
Kari Tobin, Page Production
Artistic Assistant: Richard Carbajal

Library of Congress Cataloging-in-Publication Data
Minden, Cecilia.
  Valentines for everyone / by Cecilia Minden and Joanne Meier ;
illustrated by Bob Ostrom.
    p. cm. — (Herbster readers)
  ISBN 978-1-60253-232-8 (library bound : alk. paper)
  [1. Valentine's Day—Fiction. 2. Bears—Fiction.] I. Meier, Joanne
D. II. Ostrom, Bob, ill. III. Title. IV. Series.
  PZ7.M6539Val 2009
  [E]—dc22   2009003983

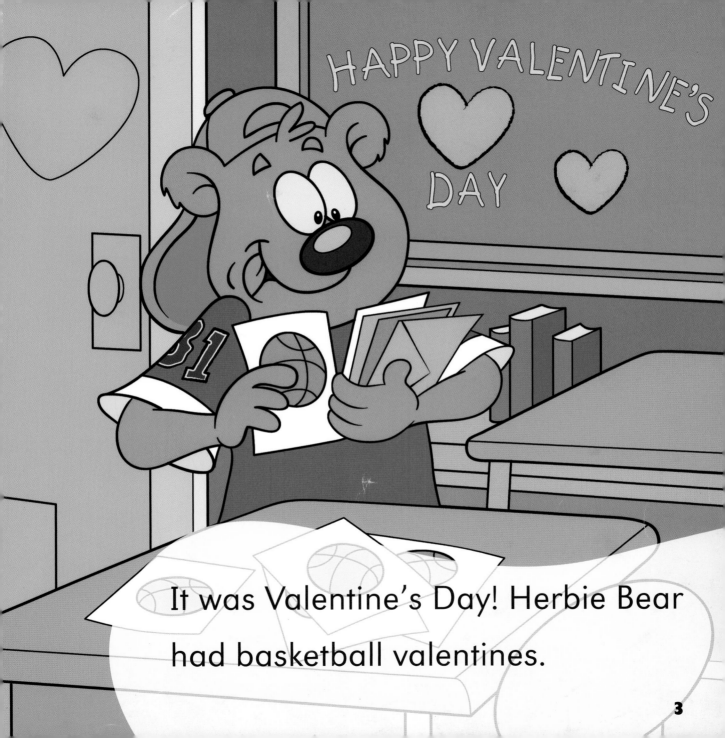

It was Valentine's Day! Herbie Bear had basketball valentines.

4

"Class," said Mr. Stone, "Meet our
new student, Maria Lamb."

5

"Hi, Maria," said the class.

"No one will have a valentine for Maria," thought Herbie. "I'd better fix that!"

Herbie made a funny card in art class.

"Now Maria will have a valentine, too," he thought.

The kids put their valentines in a box.

They were so excited!

It was hard to do any work.

At last! It was time for the party!

Mr. Stone called names
and passed out cards.

"Maria!" said Mr. Stone. He gave her Herbie's valentine.

Then he called Maria's name again.

Soon Maria's desk was piled high with cards.

Everyone had made Maria a valentine!

HAPPY VALENTINE DAY

"Thank you," said Maria. "I'm going to like this class."

28

Maria took out her own box.

"I have something for everyone, too."

The class opened their cards.

They ate valentine cookies.

The whole class had big smiles!